Bad Dog

by David McPhail

I Like to Read®

Holiday House / New York

In memory of Daisy: a good dog was she

I LIKE TO READ is a registered trademark of Holiday House, Inc.

Copyright © 2014 by David McPhail
All Rights Reserved
HOLIDAY HOUSE is registered in the U.S. Patent and Trademark Office.
Printed and Bound in November 2013 at Tien Wah Press, Johor Bahru, Johor, Malaysia.
The artwork was created with pen and ink and watercolors.
www.holidayhouse.com
First Edition
1 3 5 7 9 10 8 6 4 2

Library of Congress Cataloging-in-Publication Data
McPhail, David, 1940-
Bad dog / by David McPhail. — First edition.
pages cm. — (I like to read)
Summary: "Sometimes, Tom is a bad dog. But he can be good, too!
His family loves him no matter what" — Provided by publisher.
ISBN 978-0-8234-2852-6 (hardcover)
[1. Dogs—Fiction. 2. Behavior—Fiction.] I. Title.
PZ7.M478818Bad 2014
[E]—dc23
2012038836

Tom is my dog.
I love him.

But he can be bad.

He can make Mom mad.

He can make Dad mad.

He can make Kit mad.

Tom can be bad, bad, bad.

Dad says that Tom must go.

I am sad.

Oh, no.
Kit is gone.

Mom can't find Kit.

And Dad can't find Kit.

Tom wants me.

So I go.

I see Kit.

Mom and Dad come.
Tom is good, for now.

Tom is my dog.
I love him when he is good.
And I love him when he is bad.